A Giant First-Start Reader

This easy reader contains only 57 different words,
repeated often to help the young reader develop
word recognition and interest in reading.

Basic word list for *First Day of School*

all	hello	say
am	here	says
and	hold	school
are	hooray	shy
at	I	smiles
big	is	sneakers
car	it's	something
children	let's	sweater
Cindy	like	teacher
come	look	the
cry	me	this
day	Mother	today
door	Mother's	too
draw	my	tree
first	new	under
for	not	walks
goodbye	of	will
hall	play	with
hand	put	your

First Day of School

Written by Kim Jackson

Illustrated by Joan E. Goodman

Troll Associates

Library of Congress Cataloging in Publication Data

Jackson, Kim.
  First day of school.

  Summary: Although she is a little apprehensive at
first, Cindy enjoys her first day at school.
   1. Children's stories, American. [1. Schools—
Fiction. 2. Animals—Fiction] I. Goodman, Joan E., ill.
II. Title.
PZ7.J136255Fi   1985   [E]   84-8631
ISBN 0-8167-0359-0 (lib. bdg.)

My sneakers are new.
My sweater is, too!

Today is the first day of school.

Mother walks with me.

"Hello. Today is the first day of school!"

"Here, Cindy. Here is something
for the first day of school."

"Cindy, come play with me!"

"Not today. Today is my first day of school."

It's big. My school is big!
I hold Mother's hand.

Mother smiles at me.

The hall is big!

The door is big!

My teacher is big!

"This is Cindy," says Mother.

"Hello, Cindy!"

Look at all the children.

"This is Cindy," says the teacher.

"Hello, Cindy," say the children.

I hold Mother's hand.

Mother says goodbye.

I am shy. Will I cry?

I draw.

I draw and I draw.

"Hello, Cindy. I like your tree!"

"I like your car!" I say.

I say, "Let's put your car under my tree."

"Hooray! Today is my first day of school!"